THE ARK OF MARS

THE ARK OF MARS

by Leigh Brackett

There *are* men in space again. *The catastrophic words went out from Mars to damp Venus and frost-wracked Mercury; to the lunar colonies of Jupiter and Saturn. To all points of the system the warning was screamed:* Halt those fleeing star-pilgrims... those space-sons of the Ark of Mars.

THERE were no more men in. Space. The dark ships strod the ways between the worlds, lightless, silent, needing no human mind to guide them. The R-ships, carrying the freight and the passengers, keeping order, keeping the law, taking the Pax Terrae to the limites of the Sola System and guarding their boundary witch was not now ever to be crossed.

And there were no more men in space, no strong hands bridling the rockets, no eyes looking outward to the stars. But still upon the wide-flung worlds of Sol were old men who remembered, and young men who could dream.

The Shadow of the sandstone pillar lay black upon the ground. Kirby slipped into it and slid still looking back the way he had just come. Wilson stopped too, in the shadows, asking nervously,

"Nobody's following us, are they?"

Kirby shook his head. "I just wanted another look at the place. J don't know why, I've seen it often enough."

He had not been running. Neither he nor Wilson had been doing anything outwardly unusual, and yet Kirby was soaked with sweat and his heart was pounding. He could hear Wilson's heavy breathing, and knew it was the same with him.

I'm scared," said Wilson. "Why whould I be scared now?" He was a young man, long and narrow, with very strong, very sensitive hands.

THE ARK OF MARS

"The last time," Kirby said. "We only need a few more hours now, after all these years..."

He let his voice trail off, as though he had been going to say more and decided not to, and Wilson muttered, "You're worried about Marsh."

"He's been taking too much interest in my department lately. I wish I knew..."

"Yeah. Kirby, let's go."

"Take it easy. A minute more isn't going to matter."

The sandstone pillar, linked by chains to a line of other pillars, marked the westward limit ef the section reserved for the fliers of spaceport personnel Behind Kirby, three miles away, the geat crystal dome of Kahora rose up from the desert, glowing splendidly with light. Under its protective shell the pastel city bloomed like a hothouse garden, bathed in warmed and sweetened air. Kahora the trade City for Mars, where the business of a planet was done in luxury and comfort.

Out here where Kirby stood the everlasting wind blew thin and dry across the wastes of half a world edged with bitter dust, and the only light there was at hand came from the swift low moons. But the spaceport that served Kahora blazed with a white glare, and the control towers were tipped with crimson stars.

Kirby stood in the shadow and looked at this place where he had spent the years of his living burial since they barred the rockets out of space. And now that be was through with it, now that he was never going to see it again, the hatred that he had for it could be let free. It was a long hate, an old hate. It had lived in him like a corrosive acid, poisoning everything he did or thought. poisoning the daytimes and the night-times and even the times he spent with Shari, which were the only good ones. He wanted to be rid of it.

Wilson muttered again about going, but Kirby didn't hear him. He was looking at the shops and sheds and multifarious buildings of the port, and in particularly at the one called Parts and Supplies, which had been his personal prison.. He was looking at the looming forest of towers that controlled the dark ships, that guided them back and forth between the worlds.

He was looking at the ships.

They lay in their massive cradles, ranged rows according to type and size. The R-40 heavy freighters, the R-10 mixed carriers, the R-3 planetary patrol ships with the stings in their tails. Men worked over them. Cargo cranes rolled and rumbled, and the lights blazed. And the ships lay, cold, lofty, soulless, enduring the probing of experts into their sensitive electronic brains because they must, but obedient to nothing and answering no master but the invisible impulses of beam and power.

Above all else, Kirby hated the ships.

He was older than Wilson. He could remember Kahora Port as it had been when the rockets roared and thundered across it. He could remember the barrooms that were around it, crowded with men from every world, speaking a thousand tongues. He could remember the spacemen's talk, and how some of them were already chafing at the barrier of Pluto's orbit, finding the System too small for them and looking hungrily at the stars beyond.

He could remember. He was a rocket man. He had seen every port in the System, or most of them, before he was twenty, and at twenty-six he had his master's ticket and was waiting for a ship. He had hated the dark robots then, because some day they were going to be a threat to trade. After their initial cost, a manned rocket couldn't compete with them. But that threat seemed a long way off.

He had his master's ticket, and presently he would have a ship, and by the time the robots got themselves established, the way would be open to the stars and a whole new era would begin.

And Kirby, hating in the shadow of the sandstone pillar, thought, "But it didn't begin, the old eras caught up to us first. The wars, the booms, the busts. One war, one bust too many."

And there were no more men in space.

Wilson shuffled his feet in the blowing dust. The stolen things were weighing heavy in his pocket, and he had still to face his wife. He said, "Let's go."

Kirby looked at the dark ships. "It was the women did it," he said slowly. "Oh, some of them wore pants and shaved every day, but it was the women all the same. They wanted what women always want, peace, security, everything fixed and neat and never changing, nobody taking any risks. You can'.t blame them, I suppose. They'd had a hard time of it, but..."

Acts, Acts, Acts! Trade Stabilization. Population Stabilization. Crop Stabilization. The buisy minds of the Government working. Take the maned ships out of space, and there can't be any trade wars, any other kinds of wars. The worlds can't get at each other to fight. Stop expansion outward to the stars and there can't be any more economic upsets, any more expensive conquests, any more explosive rivelries between groups. Stabilize. Regulate. Control. Liberty is apt to be uncomfortable, let's be secure instead. The dark ships of the Government will police the Solar System. The Peace of Earth be with you!

"Inventories," said Kirby bitterly. "Do you know how many millions of inventories I've made out in that stinking Parts department?" Suddenly he laughed. "I wonder if they'll ever know how much I managed to hook out of those inventories?"

"Look," said Wilson. "Please. Let's get out of here."

Kirby shrugged and followed him. The fliers were not far away, small competent descendants of the helicopter, designed for family use like the old-fashioned automobile, and just as planet-bound. Kirby's and Wilson's were parked together. Wilson opened the door, but he didn't get in. A sudden reluctance seemed to have overtaken him.

"I thought you were in a hurry," Kirby said.

"Yeah. Damn it, Kirby, what am I going to tell her?"

"The truth."

"Oh, lord. She'll—I don't know what she'll do."

"All over Mars men are having the same trouble. Bull it through. If she screams too loud, smack her. She won't die of it."

Wilson said sourly, "It's easy for you to talk. You're a widower."

"I've got my own troubles."

"But it isn't—well, I suppose you have. But the kids, Kirby. That's the thing. That's what she'll really blow her top about."

"Listen, Wils. You knew you were going to have to do this from the beginning. It's tough on everybody, but it's too late to back out now. You believe in what you' re doing, don't you?"

"Sure. Yes. But ..."

"Then go ahead. Maybe your wife will even come around to agreeing with you some time."

Wilson said, "Ha!" very savagely. He climbed into his flier and slammed the door. Kirby stepped back. The rotors started to whir and then the small craft lifted straight up and skidded away toward the suburbs of Kahora. Kirby smiled crookedly and shook his head. He got into his own flier and took off. It ran smoothly by itself on autopilot, and he occupied his time by removing carefully from his pockets several dozen transistors he had just stolen from the government and placing them in a hidden compartment of his own designing. By the time be was finished, the blazing dome of Kahora' stood like a crystal wall on his left, showing through it a distorted vision of pastel buildings and gardens of many colors. Kirby glanced at it once. It had always seemed to him a soft, smothering place where everything, including the people, was effeminized and artificial. Like most of the resettled population, he lived outside the dome.

The suburbs were as pleasant as planning and effort could make them. Built long and low of the native clay, the houses suited the landscape and the climate. Native desert growths filled out the dry gardens. They were not lovely, but they had an exotic charm of their own, much like the Earthly cactus and the Joshua tree. Kirby had not minded the place itself, only the law that required him to live there and forbade him to leave for any length of time this particular area of Mars.

The populations of the Solar System had been carefully figured to the last decimal point and portioned out among the planets according to food and employment potentials, so that nowhere was there a scarcity or an overplus, and nobody's individual whim was allowed to upset the balance. If you wanted to change your residence from on sector or one world to another, the red tape involved was so colossal that men had been known to die of old age while waiting for a permit.

The women of the settlement toiled and wailed and nagged unceasingly to move into Kahora proper, under the dome. It was a matter of social prestige even more than of comfort. Kirby remembered that when his wife had succumbed to a mutant view that swept the colony, his first feeling had been relief that he would no longer have to hear about Kahora. He thought again of Wilson and pitied him. Trying to explain one's obvious lunacy to an irate woman was no easy task.

To Shari he would not have- to explain. He Would have only to say good-bye. Kirby stopped feeling sorry: for Wilson.

He did not turn toward the street of bungalows where he still kept a pretense of residence.

He went straight on over the low ridge behind the suburb to the Martian town that sprawled on the other side, the very ancient town that was the original Kahora. It was not so huge as it had been, showing wide abandoned fringes that crumbled slowly away into nothingness. The ruins of the King City, the old battlemented stronghold of the rulers, stood, up dark and lonely against the racing moons, and at its buttressed feet there curved the deep-gouged bed of a navigable river, dry and choked with dust. Kirby set his flier down beside a flat-roofed house on a winding narrow street, and went inside.

She was waiting for him. He had never come here in all these years that she had not been waiting for him, no matter what the hour. But tonight she was not smiling. Tonight she was not as she had ever been, and her eyes, the color of smoky topaz set a little obliquely in a high-honed face, held a look that he had never seen before, a look that did not come into the eyes of the Earth women, a fey look, wild and sombre. It made him shiver, and he started to speak, to ask her the reason for her strangeness, but she came to him swiftly and said, in the old High Martian,

"Beloved, there is danger, close behind you!"

Kirby's heart began to pound again. He reached out and caught her, almost roughly, her strong slim shoulder under his hand. "Danger, Shari? What do you mean, danger?" He paused, and then he added angrily, "What's this damned coverall you've got on? You look like the devil."

"I am going with you."

Kirby's jaw relaxed and his eyes widened. He had told her nothing.. No word had ever been said between them. And yet she— Shari, you're talking nonsense. What's the matter with you?"

"You came tonight to say goodbye."

"Who's been talking to you, Shari? Who's been telling..."

"Kirby, beloved, I am Martian I have no need for talk. The other men will force their wives to go with them because they must, but I am not your wife."

"You are. Never say that."

"But only by the custom of my people. And so you were going to leave me behind."

A fear was coming over Kirby now. He turned away from her because her eyes frightened him with the wisdom that was in them, and he said desperately, "You don't know where I'm going. You don't know what the chances are, you don't realize—"

"You are going a great distance, Kirby. Farther than men have ever gone before. I know. And if you were going farther still, I would go with you."

She had a bundle packed. He saw it, neatly rolled and tied with cords, and it was a small thing, not much to carry away into the dark beyond. He looked around suddenly at the room he knew so well, the beautiful ancient things, the priceless carpet worn thin as silk but with nothing of its brightness lost, the wide couch and the low tables carved from woods that had not grown on Mars for millenniums, the little familiar things. He said, "How long have you lived here in this house, you and your family before you?"

She smiled. "What is time on Mars? Besides, I am the last. What matter if I lose it now, or in a little while?" She put something into his hand. "It is a gun, Kirby. You will have to use it."

He stared at the unfamiliar thing, unfamiliar because it had been so many years since he had seen one, and then he looked at her sharply. "You were talking about danger."

She nodded toward the window place, where the shutters were open to the moon-light. "Listen, and you will hear it coming."

II

There was a thrumming in the sky. "Fliers," Kirby said. "Two of them." Shari picked up her bundle. "We can be away in yours before they reach here."

"No. They'd have us smack on in their radarscopes, and I don't dare lead them—" He didn't finish what he was about to say. Suddenly he shoved the gun out of sight under his loose shirt and grabbed Shari's bundle. "Peel off that coverall," he said. "Quick." There were cushions and bright silks on the couch. He hid the bundle amung them and sprawled out on top of it, a man at ease, a man without a care in the world. Shari's ugly garment vanished also among the silks. By the time the fliers droned down to a landing outside she looked as she always did, a skirt-like wrapping of pale green girdled around her hips, her breasts bare after the Martian fashion, with a collar of hammered metal plaques above them. "Fix us a drink," said Kirby, and she bent over a low table, saying softly,

"These are men from the Port, with your brother that is not of blood but of the law."

"Marsh," said Kirby, and his eyes narrowed. He said a brief malediction. Then he asked Shari, "Have you always had this—gift?" *He* tapped his forehead. "I mean, all these years you could read my mind, and I never knew it?"

She smiled. "I never used it, except to tell when you were coming. A Martian man could guard his mind, but not you. And I never told you of it because—it might have made you uncomfortable."

Kirby shook his head. "A telepath. I'll be damned. I knew Martians were supposed to have some queer powers, but I never dreamed—"

"Not all of us, Kirby, and the effort is too great to waste it on trivialities. Already my head aches." She put the tall glass in his hand

and then she kissed him briefly, fiercely, and whispered, "Be careful! And now I'll let them in."

The knocking on the door had just begun. Shari opened it, and three men came in. Two of them were government agents assigned to Port Security, and Kirby reckoned that there must be two more outside, searching his own flier. The third man was his brother-in-law. He was also Divisional Superintendent, and Kirby's superior.

Kirby sat up indignantly. "What the devil are you doing here?" he demanded. "Can't a man have any privacy?"

"I would have spoken to you at your home," said Marsh, "but of course you weren't there." He looked around the room slowly, letting his gaze slide over Shari as though she were not there. He was a tall man, He had never been muscular, and though he was not fat there were paddings of soft flesh on his cheeks and belly. His features were narrow and pronounced—very like the features of Kirby s dead wife—and his attitude, like hers, was one of deep disapproval of practically everything.

Kirby asked, "What did you have to say that couldn't be said during working hours?"

"You're under arrest."

Kirby sprang up. "Listen, a citizen still has some rights under this fine benevolent government. You'll have to do better than that. "

One of the government men stepped forward, pulling a paper out of his pocket. "Warrant," he said. "You're charged with a long lot of words, but it boils down to theft of government property, corruption of government employees, and suspicion of sabotage. That enough?"

"I guess so," said Kirby, "except that Marsh is crazy if he thinks he can pin it on me. Where's your evidence, Marsh? You can't put me in prison just because you hate my guts."

"Set your mind at rest. I have what evidence I need. But the thefts are not the important part, Kirby. It's what you're doing with the things. There's no market for them, you can't sell them anywhere—there must be another reason. I have an idea what it is, but I want you to tell me."

"You do," said Kirby, and smiled.

Marsh's thin mouth grew thinner. "I know what you're up to, whether you tell me or not, and you know what the penalty is." He came forward a little. 'I'm trying to help you, not for your sake but because you were my sister's husband, and I don't want her name involved in criminal proceedings. If you'll make a full confession, now, with the names of all other persons connected with this business, I'll withdraw my charges against you. I'll even go so far as to say that you were acting for me."

Kirby glanced at the government men. "With those two boys hanging over your shoulder? You never were very smart."

"They'll go along with me."

The government men nodded. Kirby laughed. "That important, is it? Well, I'm sorry. I don't know anything. I don't even know what you're talking about." The two men who had remained outside to search Kirby's flier came in. One of them shook his head and said, "Nothing in it." Kirby took a long drink from the glass he still held in his hand and put it down. "Marsh,'" he said, "don't you think you're letting your dislike for me carry you a little too far?"

"I don't dislike you. I'm only warning you, for your own good, to talk."

"Oh, but you do," said Kirby, moving a little to the right. "You always thought your sister was much too good for me. You know something, Marsh? Your sister was a mess. She was selfish and han-brained and trouble-making, and Mars was a better place when she left it." Underneath his words his mind was signaling frantically to Shari, "Now! Now! Can you do something to distract them?" It seemed a lunatic thing to depend on telepathy, but—

Marsh was genuinely shocked. He stared at Kirby for a moment, and then his face began to darken. He said, "You have no right to speak that way." He looked at Shari. "Especially after—" He could not bring himself to say the words. Then he snapped, "You might at least have married her!"

"I did," said Kirby. "Her people do not require laws to farce them to be faithful, They assume that where there is love there is marriage, and where there is not the whole thing had better be forgotten. We do very well."

"In that case," Marsh said acidly, "we had better arrest her too, as an accessory." He turned to the government men. "He's going to be stubborn, and we can't afford stubbornness now. Even a few hours of stalling on Kirby's part might be enough to let the ship takeoff without him."

Kirby's nerves contracted with a stabbing pain. It was no surprise to him that Marsh had guessed the truth, but he hated to hear the bald, flat mention of a thing that had been so painfully, so lovingly hidden for so long. Shari said softly, in the ceremonial High Martian that few Earthmen understood, "It is only a guess. And now I am going to speak."

One of the government men got out a flat case with a syringe in it. "I figured we'd have to loosen his tongue," he said laconically, and Kirby shivered. The truth-drugs developed since the days of scopolamine were very good. Too good. They worked.

Why the hell didn't Shari do something?

She did. She spoke suddenly and clearly in English, which she knew perfectly but almost never used. She spoke to Marsh, and her eyes were fixed on his with that queer fey look that seemed to strip his mind down naked. Kirby saw him trying to turn away from it, but he couldn't, it held him trapped. Shari said, "It is not because of your dead sister that you hate Kirby. You hate him because you are not a man."

A curious change came over Marsh's face, slight at first, so slight that Kirby hardly noticed it. He started to say something, but Shari's clear voice drowned him out. "You hate all those who love and marry, because you can find no pleasure in it. You hate courage, because you have none yourself. You are eaten up with hatred and poisoned with envy, but you are not even wicked. You are nothing."

Marsh's face had crumbled and become somehow both pitiful and repulsive. He said to Shari, "You're a liar, a filthy liar. I'm married. I have children. I—"

Shari said relentlessly, "You are not a man."

Marsh gave back a step. It seemed that he wanted desperately to evade Shari's pitiless gaze that saw everything he had hidden inside himself. He made a small whimpering sound, turning his head from side to side. The government men were all looking at Marsh now, and not at Kirby. One of them snickered, and Marsh winced, drawing back his lips in the grimace of a child about to cry. Kirby took his eyes away from Marsh. He was inexpressibly shocked. He had always had a healthy detestation for his brother-in-law, but he wished that Shari had not done this. Then the reason for her doing it came back to him, and he pulled the gun from underneath his shirt.

"All right," he said. "Everybody stand still. Get your hands up."

Immediately be was the center of attention. For a second or two nobody did move, stricken with astonishment at the sight of the gun. They had never dreamed that be might be armed. Nobody was armed any more. It was unheard of. Even the government police carried only shockers that stunned but did not kill. Kirby was grateful to whatever male relative of Shari's it had been who buried this forbidden relic of the bad old days in the Martian city of Kahora.

"It shoots bullets," he said, so that they should all understand. "It was built to be lethal, not polite, and my marksmanship is very rusty. I couldn't guarantee just to cripple you. Starting one by one from the left, will you move away from the door? Shari, close the shutters."

Uncertainly, looking at each other as men do who are momentarily at a loss and hoping for an example from somebody else, Marsh and the Government men began to move. Kirby heard the shutters bang, and then Shari came up beside him. The man with the drug-case was still holding it in his upraised hand. Kirby said, "You. let it drop."

Shari cried, "He'll throw it."

Kirby ducked. The hard case flashed past his head. The man reached fast for the shocker that was holstered under his armpit. Kirby fired. The gun made a very loud noise. The man doubled up and sat down on the floor. Kirby saw movement among the others. He fired again, and missed, but the bullet whined close between two heads, and the movement stopped. Marsh had turned an ashen gray. He leaned against the wall, not saying anything, waiting to be sick. Kirby did not feel so well himself. He kept glancing at the man who was rocking back and forth over his knees and sobbing.

"He is not dying," Shari said, answering his thought. "It is only that he does not care for pain. Keep them still while I bind them."

They were ready to be still now. Shari laughed. "They do not love the government enough to die for it. They are all thinking that they have done their best, and now it is up to others." Her hands worked swiftly. Suddenly she stopped. "Kirby, they are thinking that the R-3 ships will track you down and destroy you and all the others."

"Go ahead, tie them up." Kirby went and stuck the muzzle of the gun close to Marsh's face. "Have the R-3's been alerted?"

"Yes. You can't escape them, Kirby. They'll find your ship, they'll smash it up, they'll smash you and all the others, and there won't be any mercy..."

He was screaming like a woman. Kirby hit him across the mouth, not out of vengefulness but to stop the ugly noise Shari said quietly, "He lies. It is done now, Kirby. Come."

She found her bundle and her coverall, bunching them together under her arm. Kirby went with her out the door, shutting it carefully behind them. The shots had not attracted any crowd. He had not thought they would. The Martians had a way of letting Earthmen handle their own troubles without interference.

Kirby walked fast toward the fliers "What about the R-3's, Shari? Could you read his mind?"

"The authorities are waiting at the port. They thought there would be no trouble about handling you, but they knew that it might take a little time if the drugs had to be used. They know you're here, of course—Marsh told them when he landed."

"Yeah. We have some leeway, then?"

"Until at the port they begin to wonder why no further report has been made." She put her hand to her head and pressed it. "I wish I were better at this. My brain is cracking open."

Kirby hesitated, looking at the three craft and scowling. Then he thrust Shari into his own and said, "I'll be back in a second. Maybe I can stall 'em a while longer."

His own communicator would not operate on the official UHF band, which was closed to civilians. He climbed into one of the other fliers and bent over the radio. Then he hesitated again, overcome by a sudden desire to let well enough alone. For precious seconds he stood there fingering the switch, trying to make up his mind. "Bull by the horns," he muttered at last. He was afraid of the R-3's. Any risk was worthwhile if it held them back a little longer. He began to search his pockets. "Damn it, I never have a handkerchief. Oh, well, this'll do." He hauled out his shirttail and wrapped it over his mouth, Then he opened the switch and spoke, pitching his voice a bit high. "Port Security. This is Marsh, calling Port—"

"Receiving you. What's going on?'

Kirby's voice cracked from sheer nervousness, giving an impression of excitement he could not have counterfeited. "Everything's fine. Kirby put up more resistance than we looked for, but he's under the drugs now and as soon as they take effect we'll have the whole story."

"Good. What about the woman?" Kirby sniffed. "You know her kind. I'm going back in the house now—I don't want to miss anything. We'll keep you posted."

"Right, Remember, we want the information as soon as you get it. We're ready to act as soon as we have anything to go on."

Kirby mumbled something about patience and it wouldn't t be long now. Port Security Signed off. Kirby closed the switch, remembering some big stones that lay on the ground outside, He got one and went to work with it, in a violent hurry. When he was through both official communicators and both flight control panels were out of commission. If Marsh and the others should get free it would not do them any immediate good.

Shari was waiting quietly. She said nothing while he lifted off and sent his flier rushing at full power along an oblique course that led out over the desert She seemed very tired, and there were lines of pain around her mouth. Kirby leaned over and kissed her.

"You can rest now. You've saved us this time."

She shook her head and sighed. "I'll have to. My mind is tired. Until I've slept it will be useless."

With more control over her nerves than Kirby could have mustered, she slid down in the padded seat and slept, almost at once. He looked at her. Since the decision had been hers, unsought and unsuggested, he was glad she had come. She was too much a part of him to be left behind now, and there was another reason, too. The whole venture had shifted abruptly into a sharper focus. He was savagely determined that it had to succeed, all the way, because nothing must happen to Shari.

The desert reeled away beneath them, mile on empty mile, with nothing to break its desolation but an occasional wandering dust-devil. The moons sank out of sight. Once Kirby saw in the distance the black line of a canal with a town beside it, pricked out with a scattering of torches. The Earth-man's civilization did not rear this far into the heart of Mars. There was only timelessness out here, and a long slow dying. The stars burned magnificently overhead in the thin dry air. Kirby studied them with a kind of intimacy. He was afraid, and yet he felt as he had not felt in years, not since he was a green kid stepping away from Earth for the first time, outbound for strange new worlds.

He pushed the flier to the limit of its speed, and it was fast, but there was not time enough given to him, and he knew that there would not be. He had still a long way to go when the urgent signal from his own communicator shrilled through the cockpit. A second or two later a man's harsh voice called out his own name, and added, "Acknowledge at once!"

Kirby did not acknowledge. There was nothing be wanted to say, and he was not going to oblige them with a carrier wave so they could fix his position. He waited. "This is your last warning, Kirby. Your only chance is to obey instructions immediately. The R-3's have been sent out."

III

SHARI had wakened. She straightened up and looked at Kirby. Shall we be able to make it?"

"I don't know. Depends on how long it takes the R-3's to locate us. They'll have to hunt, and there's a lot of desert around Kahora. On the other hand, they're fast. A hell of a lot faster than we are."

He looked around apprehensively, but their was no sign of anything yet in the sky, nor did his radarscope show any warning pip, Shari put her hand over on top of his.

"I think perhaps luck will be with us," she said. "You're afraid now, but it is mostly for me. Don't be. Whatever happens, it could not have been any other way."

He took her hand and squeezed it savagely. "I'll see to it nothing does happen. Damn it, this desert always did seem to go on forever. Won't those blasted mountains ever show?"

It seemed to Kirby that the flier barely moved. His heart thumped painfully, and every nerve ending was awake and leaping . He hunched over the controls, trying to urge the small craft forward as one does a horse, with his own body. And then Shari said a surprising thing. She said, "For the first time since I have known you, you are happy."

"Happy!" he said. He laughed.

"But you are. I think it's because for the first time you feel free. The net is broken. You may die, but you will not again be a prisoner."

He grunted. "I wouldn't know. Right now I don't feel anything at all but scared." Ahead of him, out of the gloom, there lifted a jagged wall—not high, because the ceaseless tramping of the centuries had worn away the soil, and then the softer rock, and then the hard rock, grinding them into powdery dust to roll away with the wind, so that only a tag and a bone of a mountain chain was left. But it was the thing Kirby was looking for. He shouted suddenly, and on the heels of his exultance like a jeering echo came the first monotonous peet-peet-peet from the radarscope, and a bright little pip showed up at the edge of the screen.

"The mountains are close," said Shari.

"So's the R-3. And look at it come!"

The bright pip moved like a shooting star across the screen. The intensity of the single note increased rapidly. Kirby groaned. The gnawed and ancient peaks were not ahead of him now, but underneath, and the place he wanted to get to was so agonizingly near at hand—

His communicator clamored at him suddenly. It was the port Control Center, where the men with the dials and the indicators and the screens and the infinite numbers of gadgets controlled the R-ships, guiding them, receiving data from them, making the decisions and the final pushings of the ultimate buttons.

"You're centered, Kirby. You have ten seconds before the proximity trip releases the first missile—unless we stop it. You're Being given one more chance. Acknowledge! One—two—three—four—"

Kirby glanced aside at Shari. Then he reached out fast and, clicked over the switch. "Kirby acknowledging!. This is Kirby—hold your fire!"

"All right. Here's the deal. We want the star-ship, and we want it now, right away, fast. We know you're close to it. Lead on, and we'll smash it up instead of you."

"What happens to me afterward?" asked Kirby sullenly.

"You'll be alive. So will the person you have with you. You haven't anything to lose, and you know we'll get the star-ship anyway."

"Then why make deals with me?"

"We'd rather get it on the ground, before there's even an attempt at taking off. Psychological reasons."

Kirby glared at the passing peaks beneath him, lines drawn deep between his brows. At last he said heavily, "It's in a cleft of the sea-bottom, about seventy miles ahead."

"Good. We thought you'd see reason, As soon as the R-3 picks it up visually we'll notify you to turn around and come home."

"All right." Kirby's voice rose to a sharper edge. "I just want you to know that I'm not giving up for myself, I'd just as soon get blown to hell as live like a kept woman any longer. But you're right, I've got somebody with me."

"It all adds up to the same thing. Go ahead, Kirby, but be very careful. That proximity trip is all ready to go the minute anything looks wrong."

"Don't get impatient," Kirby snorted. "I'm right on course. Seventy miles."

"We're patient people. And leave your communicator open,"

Kirby turned to Shari. She was leaning toward him, toward the microphone. Her eyes were very bright. Abruptly, in a shrill loud tone that was not like her usual voice at all, she began to upbraid him, calling him a coward, a weakling, an old woman, and going on from there in Low Martian to language he would not have thought she knew. He answered her back; sulkily at first and then more and more angrily, until they were shouting at one other and the narrow confines or the cabin rang with it. Faintly from the speaker Kirby could hear the man at Control Center laughing. Moving as silently as he could he slid out of the seat and opened his secret hiding place and shifted the precious transistors into his pockets. The night beyond the cabin winow showed intensely dark Shari's voice pealed on, rising to a fish-wifely frenzy. He roared back at her, using out of three vocabularies every dirty word he could lay his tongue to, and handed her her rolled-up bundle. Then he reached over and shoved a lever on the panel. The flier lurched. A volley of deafening explosions broke out and the starboard wing rotor went crazy. Shari screamed, "Do something, you fool, Y0tl idiot! We're going to crash..."

Kirby yelled into the microphone, "Hold back your damn robot, I've got to slow down!"

"What's wrong?"

"Are you deaf or something? I've been pushing this crate too hard and she's hot and she's jammed." Kirby fought the controls, grinning, the sweat pouring down his face. He nodded to Shari. Under cover of the racket the motor was making she opened the cockpit door, never once pausing in her maniacal shrieks. "I'm slowing down," Kirby told Control Center. "Don't run over me. Damn you, Shari, shut up!" He brought his palms together hard with a cracking sound. She let out one last yip and was quiet, crouching by the open door, the wind whipping her silken skirt around her legs.

Control Center said, "We're synchronizing speed. Can you clear your motor?"

Kirby worked the lever. The motor choked, roared for a minute into life, and then choked again. There were further explosions. He throttled down some more and made another adjustment. The motor coughed and began to chug along quite normally. Kirby said, "Yeah. But I'll have to take it easy and let her cool. There's no hurry anyway." The worn eroded heap of mountain below was gashed with shallow valleys, welling now with darkness. Kirby had lost altitude along with speed. The ridges and plateaus that walled the valleys in were not too far below, not much farther than a man could jump if he wasn't afraid to take a chance.

"Listen, Kirby," said the voice from Control Center grimly, "if that ship takes off before we reach it, the deal's no good. You understand that."

"They won't. tack off without me, not if they can help it."

"Why are you so important?"

"You don't realize what a rare commodity I am." Kirby was very still now, very tense. His eyes moved sharply from the instrument panel to the black night ahead, and then back again. The flier was going by itself now on autopilot. His right hand was raised, and Shari watched it, crouching by the open door. Kirby said to the microphone, "In this day and age, an experienced spaceman with a master's rating who's still young enough to move without creaking is worth his weight in diamonds to the right people. You bet I'm important."

A dim plateau slid out of the darkness, close underneath. Kirby counted under his breath, and then his upraised hand flashed down, Before the gesture was finished, Shari jumped.

"Is that why you got into this, Kirby to be important, to be a spaceman again?"

"Oh, hell," said Kirby, "what difference does it make now? All I wind up being is a Judas goat, and inside of an hour the ship will be a pile of junk. Just be content with what you've got and don't worry about motives." He made a dial setting on the autopilot. "Another five minutes and I can increase speed again, if that'll make you any happier."

"Kirby..."

"Oh, shut up. This is bad enough without having to yak about it."

"Okay, if that's the way you want it."

Silence.

Kirby rose and crept to the door and jumped.

He had waited almost too long. The plateau was not wide, and he hit so close to the drop-off that he thought he was going to go over. He lay flat on the rock, jarred to his back teeth by the brief fall, and watched his flier buzzing purposefully away on its course. The small plateau was the last jut of the mountains. Here they fell away into a great deep gulf that had held an inland sea as big as the Caspian, in the days before Mars began to die.

He lay still, watching, and presently above him a shadow passed. It passed without sound not twenty feet over his head, as a shark passes over a swimmer in deep water, dark, unhurried, huge, and potent with a devouring fury. The starlight touched its tapering flanks with a cold pale glimmer and brought to the lensed "eyes" on its forward surface an eerie glint of life. Kirby knew that those eyes were no more than electronic cameras, and that they were blinded by the dark—when they needed to "see" the powerful floodlights would click on and give them day, but they were not looking for anything yet. Even so, he shrank closer to the rock, fighting off a horrid conviction that this unnatural child of the guided missile and the pilotless plane was a living thing, sentient, all powerful and eager to slay.

It went on, leaving only a whisper of air behind it, following the flier. It pleased Kirby to think of the very small robot innocently betraying its savage cousin. He got up off the rock, calling for Shari, and a man's voice spoke to him out of the darkness.

"Kirby! Kirby, is that you?"

"Yeah." He made out a nervous shadow and went toward it, recognizing it as Hockley, a power installation technician from a secondary spaceport over on the other, side of Mars. Hockley was crouching beside a heap of carefully arranged stones that concealed a field telephone, permanent equipment on this lookout post, and somebody was talking over the phone in a way that verged on the hysterical, but Hockley was paying no attention to it. He was staring after the dark ship.

Kirby took the phone. He spoke into it briefly, giving the exact coordinates of the course being taken by the flier and the R-3. Then he said, "Is everybody accounted for?"

The voice on the other end said, "Now that you're here. You're late."

"Get 'em all strapped in. We're coming down."

"Make it fast!"

Kirby put the phone away and shouted again for Shari. She had come up quietly while he talked and was standing beside him, waiting. They started off, the three of them, down the broken, tumbled path that twisted to the foot of the long slope. Both men had made the trip many times before. Sliding and skidding on the steep stretches, raising a trail of fine dust, they went down the drop at a speed that was not quite reckless, alternately helping Shari. On both sides of the path there stretched curious mounds and heaps of stone, a few of them still betraying a rectangular shape. Looking at them, Shari said abruptly, "This was once a city."

Kirby nodded. "It was a port, until the sea dried up and left it." He stopped suddenly, digging his heels in the dust. Out over the sea-bottom a tiny nova had burst and died.

"That," said Kirby, "was my flier. Control Center is not so dumb as I had hoped.

Hockley said something between a curse and a prayer. "It'll come back now, looking for us."

A Shaft of light, distant but blinding bright, appeared like a pillar upon the desert. It moved. Hockley groaned and Bung himself on down the path. Kirby was right on his heels.

They passed the harbor quays, huge broken Monoliths worn round and shapeless, still lying dutifully along the edges of a deep gorge that had once been filled with blue water but was now only a naked gash in the rock. There was a way down the cliff, a way like a broad stair. Men had made it, men who had still followed the shrinking sea. Fishermen, probably, climbing down to their boats. The mouths of great caverns yawned beside it, holes gnawed out of the cliff in ages gone by the action of the water. The two men and woman ran, their feet clattering on the stone. The bright pillar moved swiftly over the sea-bottom, light for the R-3's searching "eyes." In the darkness on the floor of the dry harbor there was hurried movement, and a sound of voices, and a glinting of the cold stars off of colder metal.

Hockley said, "I wish we had more of those. I wish we had a thousand."

"One ought to be enough,"

There was a flash, a hiss, and a nerve-chilling whine that vanished away almost before it was heard. Kirby stopped running, holding tight to Shan's hand. Hockley stopped. They stood motionless. Seconds crawled by like years, and nothing happened. Hockley whispered, "They missed..."

"They couldn't they had the course." Besides those babies can find their own target, that's what they're built for, to intercept..."

A second nova, vastly larger, flared and fell, and after an interval came the shock-wave and the noise. Kirby laughed.

"Control Center wasn't expecting that. Now we go!"

They half fell the rest of the short way to the bottom. A little group of men recived them. The portable rack from which they had launched the interceptor missile had already been shoved aside, out of the way. All together they plunged into a vast lopsided opening in the cliff as high as two cathedrals. There were lights in there, carefully shaded so that no gleam reached out-side. There were numerous fliers, parked together in a bay of the cavern. Around the walls there were forges and machine tools, collected painfully piece by piece over the years, improvised, patched together. There was the litter of much working. There was a ship.

Shari uttered a small cry of surprise. "But it's so ugly!"

"What did you expect?" snapped Kirby. "An ex-tramp freighter..."

She laughed. "I'm sorry. But in your mind its image has been clothed with such beauty!"

They stumbled up the gangplank, crowding the narrow lock that had over its inner door the faded letters, LUCY B. DAVENPORT, TERRA. Inside there was pandemonium. Men were shouting. An uproar of women's voices filled all the spaces within the hull, punctuated by the bawlings of the of children. The outer door of the lock clanged shut. Kirby gave Shari's hand a final squeeze and left her to shift for herself. He, too, began to shout, running forward along the corridor. Somebody heard him and got hold of the intercom, ordering everyone to shut up and prepare for take-off. Nobody seemed to pay much attention. It still sounded to Kirby like riots going on all over the ship. He clattered up the ladder into the bridge and slammed the door behind him. It was quieter. "Ger the hell out of there, Pop," he. said to the old man who was sitting in the pilot chair.

Pop Barstow grinned at him. "I was hoping you wouldn't show up, so's I could take the old Aak off myself. He slid into the copilot's place and laid the webbing over his lank middle.

Kirby said grimly, "You may get your chance yet. Give 'em the siren." He punched the firing keys. A great roaring filled the cavern and the deck beneath him leaped a little. The siren began to wail. The ship's bow-light came on, outlining the cavern's mouth in a hard white brilliance. Sitting stiff and quivering in the pilot's chair, Kirby began to nurse the *Lucy Davenport* forward along the way that had been prepared for her. It had been a long time since he held a ship under his hands. Too long. He was scared. Maybe he'd lost his touch. Maybe he couldn't do it any more. Maybe he'd crash her, with all those screaming women and kids....With Shari.

"Butterflies?" asked Barstow.

Kirby shook his head. "Sea gulls."

"You're too young, Kirby. Let me have her."

Kirby laughed. They were clear of the cavern now—almost. A little way more. His insides felt as though they were caught in a vise. They hurt.

Shaw, the radarman, said suddenly, "I'm picking up something." from the back of the bridgeroom where he bent over the 'scope there came the monotonous, nerve-clawing bleat of the signal, still faint but growing louder.

"More R-3's," said Barstow. "Well, young Kirby, are you going to let 'em catch us."

They were clear now. Kirby shut his jaws together and leaned forward over the control bank. The belly jets cut in with a howl and a burst of flame. The ship rose up enormously as though on a column of fire, and the stern jets opened wide to full power. The *Lucy B. Davenport* pointed her nose to the black sky and went up screaming, leaving behind her a roll of apocalyptic thunder. Almost before Kirby knew it they were in silence and open space, and the radarscope was blank.

Pop Barstow reached solemnly inside his shirt and came out with a bottle. He drank and passed it to Kirby, who needed it.

"Well," said Barstow, "so far, so good. We made it."

33

THE ARK OF MARS

Kirby gasped and ran his hand over his mouth, passing the bottle back. He looked out through the bow port. The landing light was off, and there was space, where he had lived once until he was prisoned on a planet. It had not changed. The stars burned just as bright, and the gulfs between them were as deep and dark and cold. He shivered, a shallow twitching of the skin. He was a stranger here now, an intruder. Space no longer belonged to men. It was the kingdom of the dark ships, of which the R-3's had been only the small foretaste.

At her present desperate rate of acceleration the *Lucy Davenport* would be clear of the System and beyond the range of the interplanetary control stations before even the Mars-based ships could catch her. They had timed their take-off very carefully for that. From then on there was nothing between them and their destination but space—4.3 light-years of it.

But even in the immensity of interstellar space there was no safety. Here, too, the dark ships had outstripped man. It was only a question of time....

"Yeah," said Kirby heavily, "we made it. Now all we have to do is wait and wonder every second if the R-ships' can run us down,"

IV

The word went out from Mars: *There are men in space again.*

Secretly and stealthily that word went, on the tight Government beams, but it was heard and repeated. Inward from Mars it traveled, across Earth and Venus and into the sun-bitten, frost-wracked valleys of Mercury. Outward from Mars it traveled, to the lunar colonies of Jupiter and Saturn, to the nighted mining-camps of the worlds beyond . *There are men in space again!*

Human mind and muscle had challenged the dark ships, and the barriers that had been so strong were broken, the frontiers that bad been dosed were open, and a thing had been done so splendid and insane and terrifying that it struck the mass consciousness with the impact of a bomb.

There was no longer any point in feigning secrecy. The news services broadcast the story, training expressive cameras on the comfortable houses left vacant and forlorn, the abandoned toys, the supper dishes still untouched on dusty tables.

Neighbor women shook their heads for a System-wide audience, lamenting the tragic fate of those whose husbands and fathers had so forcibly betrayed them. Two prospective passengers who had fled screaming into the night, leaving their husbands to go starward alone, gave solom interviews and received much sympathetic attention. To that portion of the population given to feeling intensely about things, the *Lucy B. Davenport* became a symbol.

To most she was the black shadow of reaction, the last resurgence of the bad old days. To some, chiefly the boys and the young men with dreams not quite stamped out of them yet, she was the bright single spark in a dreary monotone. If she made it, she would have started something. If she made it, she would have ended something, too-the absolute authority of the dark ships.

THE ARK OF MARS

If she made it.

Here and there, scattered through the Solar System, certain men—other Kirbys and Wilsons and Pop Barstows—had a special interest in the outcome. The *Lucy B. Davenport* was not the only survivor of the Age of Rockets, cherished in the secrecy of waste places. It was not possible that she could have been. The law requiring the surrender and destruction of all manned ships was a challenge to the rebellious old Adam inherent in the human race. A few men actually succeeded in breaking it.

On Pluto there was activity. There was a base there for the heavily-shielded R-40's that carried the uranium ore from the mines. Behind it there were black mountains sheathed in ice, and all around it was a plain that glittered in the starlight, white with frozen air. The base itself was one vast sunken dome, for the ships and for the men that served them. But to one side was a second dome, and above it was a group of towers somewhat different from those of the base proper, squatter and more massive. This place had been used once. Since then it had lain quiet, its contents sheathed cocoon-like in protective webs.

Now men invaded it again, stripping away the sheathing, checking, testing, making delicate adjustments. And underneath the dome the giant dynamos awoke, and the solid granite of the plain was shaken.

On its massive launching truck, a long dark shape lay waiting.

Far out in the gulf that lies between Sol and Alpha Centauri Kirby wished desperately that he had never been born. "Can't they shut up?" he demanded of Pop Barstow. "Don't they ever shut up?"

"Ain't the nature of the beast," said Pop, who had three wives. He added philosophically, "Have a drink."

Kirby swore. "How many bottles did you smuggle aboard? Anyway, that's not the answer. I don't mind them yakking. I don't even mind them screaming. It's what they're doing to the men. Rotting the hearts out of them, that's what they're doing! Making 'em more like rabbits every day. They—"

"You can't blame them too much," said Shari gently. She was curled up in a corner of the bench that ran around part of the bridge, looking tired, looking bored, looking infinitely, infuriatingly patient. "It wasn't their idea to come."

"I don't know why you want to defend them," said Kirby irritably, "after the way they've treated you." He knew she was right, but it only angered him more to know it. He turned to Pop Barstow. "They think Shari isn't decent. Can you beat that?"

Pop grinned. "You don't know the ladies very well, do you, young Kirby? It isn't her morals they care about, one way or the other. It's her looks. Ain't that so, Shari?"

She nodded, looked at Kirby, smiling. "Now you see why I haven't been angry with them."

Kirby rose. "I give up." He stood frowning a little absently in Shari's direction. Then he said, "You're still not sorry you came?"

"Don't you go back on me, that's all. I'd jump right out the window." He kissed her, and said, without joy, "Well, I suppose I better go down and talk to them."

"Luck," said Pop cynically. He had had three wives.

Kirby went out and down the passage. One watch before the ark had reached the maximum acceleration her middle-aged bones could stand, and the stern rockets had been cut. She was running now on constant velocity, in absolute silence except when one of the auxiliaries was cut in briefly by the automatic compensators to keep her dead on course, or by the sensor-field detector relays to avoid spatial debris. After the incessant roaring he had become used to, Kirby's own footsteps sounded unnaturally loud in the stillness. He didn't like it. It gave him a feeling of cessation, of not moving, when every nerve was screaming to make speed, speed, and more speed. He wished that somebody had perfected one of those interstellar drives they had talked about, and that he had it. Might as well wish for wings. Or luck. All he had was an elderly ship and conventional rockets, and it was going to be a long trip. Unless it was a very short one.

He went down a winding ladder to the cargo deck. It ceased to be silent. The main holds below were full of everything they had been able to latch onto and smuggle out in the fliers, added onto the original cargo the ark had been carrying when she went into hiding. But the cargo deck had been cleared of what light stuff was in it and refilled with women and kids.

Every one of them, Kirby thought, was yelling at full lungpower. Babies cried. Small children roared—in pleasure or pain, it was impossible to tell which. Half a dozen teen-aged girls giggled together in a corner. A boy the same age was shooting paper wads at them. Women moved here and there, doing things, doing nothing, or sat still on the improvised bunks, or smacked their young ones. There was a faint odor of cooking.

A network of cords ran overhead, with blankets and tarpaulins fixed to them, so that the separate families might have some privacy when they wanted it. Some of the cords were hung with diapers, and rows of little pants and shirts, and feminine under-garments. The husbands and fathers who were off duty and had no place else to go were scattered here and there, looking dismal, like men who have been beaten for a very long time: Wilson was among them. He sat humped over beside a bunk on which his wife lay in the attitude of an uncompromising corpse, staring straight. Up at roof.

Kirby he hesitated, trying to think if there wasn't something vital he had to see to in the Bridgeroom. But it was too late. He was spotted. The riot began.

He had managed to avoid this so far. He and Shari, with Pop and what single men there were aboard, bunked in the officers' cabins on the bridge deck, and his duty had given him an excuse to ignore the requests forwarded to him from below to come down and be slain. For some reason the women seemed to have fastened on him as the arch-demon, probably because he made the actual flying possible, and because he was by circumstance placed in supreme authority as skipper of this reluctant star-ark. He climbed part way up the ladder again and roared for silence.

Wilson's wife got up off her bed and stalked through the crowd until she was directly below Kirby. The gabble of voices quieted somewhat, enough that he could hear her quite plainly.

"You don't have anything to say to us that we want to hear. Phil Kirby!" she said, snapping each separate word off with an audible click of her teeth. She wasn't at all bad looking. Kirby had always liked her. Now he had an almost uncontrollable urge to lay her over his knee and give her something to complain about.

She moved a little doser, showing the whites of her eyes. "All we want is to be taken home again. And if there was any body but you fit to fly us home, we'd—we'd—" Words formed a hard lump in her throat and choked her. She moved forward again. "You got my Wils into this, you crazy good-far-nothing Squaw-man! He'd never have done it if you..."

The flat of Kirby's hand shut off the rest of it. He had come down off the ladder and his face was perfectly white. Sally Wilson whimpered and put her fingers over her mouth, staring at him as though the sky had fallen.

Wilson moved forward, not angry but pretending he was angry because he had to, and said, "Here now, Kirby! Even if Sally was out of line, you can't—"

Kirby said quietly, "Shari is my wife. I'll have no such talk about her." He looked around the circle of lades. "Is that understood?" A pudding-faced girl in the back row started to say something, and he bellowed, "Shut up!" He glared at them all impartially, and then turned again to Sally Wilson. "Why is it you women always think everybody but yourselves is a spineless moron without a will of his own, wide open to be led into anything? I got your Wils into this, did I? Here, you, Wilson! And Hockley, and Weiss—all you guys! Did I lead you into anything, or did you damn well get into this of your own free will?"

Wilson scuffed the toe of his boot on the deck, evading Kirby's eyes. "Aw," he said, "you know how—"

"Did you or didn't you?"

Wilson thrust out his lip like a rebellious small boy and said loudly, "Yes! Yes, I did. And so did all the rest of us."

A chorus of male voices added assent .

"Good," said Kirby. "Then that's settled. And—"

A very large young woman with an enormous pink child in her arms thrust herself in front of Kirby and said, "I don't care whose idea it was, it wasn't mine, and I want to go home." Quite suddenly she thrust the child at him. "Look at her," she demanded. "Look at this poor little innocent helpless baby. Can you stand there and tell me that you don't care what happens to her."

The child, alarmed by the uproar, began to howl and kick Kirby in the stomach. The mother grabbed it back. "No, I can see you don't care. You don't care if we die on this horrible old Ship, or get torn to pieces by wild animals on some world nobody ever heard of. It's men like you that made a mess out of everything before, and you'd do it again, you wouldn't care what happened to other people, just so you could satisfy your crazy whims."

She raised her voice another notch. "I want to go home. I demand to go home! We all demand to go home!"

Kirby waited until he could make himself heard again. Then he shook his head. "You women are funny. You all loved your husbands enough to start this journey with them, and now you want to turn back."

"We were forced to come! We—"

"No, you weren't. Not actually. You could have screamed for help and had your husbands put safely away in the Plutonian mines for life. But you didn't—you chose to come. Now it seems you're sorry you didn't have them sent to Pluto, so you could stay with your little curtains and your tea-sets and the pretty cruddies on the mantel. all the really important things."

Sally Wilson began to cry. "But we were all so happy where we were. Why did you have to do this? What more could you want that you didn't have?"

Kirby said soberly. "If you don't know, it wouldn't be any use to tell you." He looked at the children. They were quiet now, awed by the sound and, fury, standing in little mobs and staring. "Maybe it was for them, more than anything. They ought to have a chance to grow up to be men and women, not just numbers on a big sheet of statistics. Besides," he added with sudden intensity, "it has to be now. Pretty soon there won't be anybody left who can handle a ship, and it'll be too late. People will sit in their dull comfortable little nests and stagnate and rot and get softer every year, and that'll be the end of us. You know the real thing that's being taken out of us? Youth.

Kids are born and brought up already middle-aged. There aren't any horizons any more. Just comfort."

"I like comfort," said the large young woman defiantly.

"Well, you're fed three meals a day, there's a roof over your head and no rent to pay, so why worry? Listen, we've got a long voyage ahead of us. Let's not make it any tougher on ourselves."

The large young woman snorted. "I'm sure," she said nastily, "that we're all anxious to make things pleasant for you."

"You better," Kirby snarled, "because if anyone of you makes trouble I'll slam you right into the brig. Believe me, the only reason you're here is biological. Women, unfortunately, are a necessary adjunct to colonization."

He turned to climb the ladder again, and then some underlying twinge of pity made him turn again and say, "Don't think about what you've left behind. Think about what's ahead. It's a beautiful world. Very much like Earth. You can have your pick of places to live. It isn't inhabited. You can make new towns a whole new country, just to suit yourselves. There'll be others along too. We're not the only ones who still think freedom wasn't so bad. Your kids will grow up to be the lawmakers of a new world, the pioneers of a galactic civilization."

It sounded fine when he said it. He hoped it would work out that way.

Someone said, "You don't know what it's like, there any more than we do. Nobody's ever been there. What's the use of lying about it?"

Kirby groaned. "I thought that had been explained to you. All right, I'll give it to you again. Years ago the Government built a special long-range base on Pluto and sent out from it a robot star-ship. It was strictly a reconnaissance flight. They wanted to know what was out there, and whether it held any threat to System security. The data the

R-ship brought back were never made public, naturally. But those things have a way of getting out. I've seen clips from the films taken by automatic cameras and photostats of data concerning atmosphere, gravity, temperatures, the works. Alpha Centauri has an A-1 habitable planet. Does that satisfy you?"

"I'll believe it," said the large young woman, "when I see it. In the meantime how long will we be shut up in this smelly old trap?"

"Well," said Kirby uncomfortably, "quite a while."

"That's no answer. Weeks? Months? Years?"

"Years. About five of them. Our velocity is something under the speed of light—"

Too much under. The R-ships are faster. The question is, do we have enough head start? Once we land, we'll be safe—scatter out and hide—a planet's a big place. But if we miscalculated, if they overhaul us—

"Five years. Five *years?*"

Kirby said, "We've got supplies, if we're careful with them. We've got a doctor and a nurse and you're all in good health. We—"

But suppose we did miscalculate, and suppose our emergency plan doesn't work? Suppose something goes wrong with the ship, with the air supply, or the water, or suppose we're hulled by a hunk of drift too big to patch up, after. And then, oh God, what will we have done? The women had a choice, maybe. But the kids no,

He looked at the fat child straddling the large young woman's ample hip. It stared back at him, pop-eyed, smearing tears over its face with a grubby palm. Its nose was running. It snuffled, and Kirby was overcome with awe and horror and a sense of guilt.

Somebody shrieked in anguish, "Five years? You mean that for five long solid years I've got to stay in this room with certain people I wouldn't associate with—"

Voices.

"Joe Zimmerman, what did you mean, telling me it wouldn't take long? Joe, you come back here and answer me—"

"But I didn't bring nearly enough clothes—"

"—no decent kitchen, and those awful beds—"

"—no real privacy, you can hear every word that's said, it's indecent!"

"—have a baby *here?*"

"How could you dare to get me into this?"

Bedlam.

Kirby fled up the ladder, clapped the hatch shut, and made it fast. When the men, such as were left alive, came on watch again, somebody else could let them out.

He went back to the bridge. Pop started to say something, and thought better of it. Kirby went over to Shari and put his two hands on her shoulders. "Women are fine," he said. "I have nothing against them. But if you ever start acting like one, I'll break your neck."

Pop Barstow laughed. "Son," he said, "you don't know it, but you have only just begun to fight. "

V

In the gulf that runs from Sol to Alpha Centauri there were now two ships. One was far ahead, but the second ship was possessed of an infinite patience and a greater speed. With every space-league the gap between them grew a little smaller.

On the second ship t here was silence within and without. Nothing human lived in it. There was no need of anything human. The ship was sufficient unto itself.

From its dark hull the sensor field spread wide, infinitely sensitive, tirelessly inquisitive. It touched an object, plunging nearer on an oblique course. Through its external contact-points the sensor-field transmitted a series of impulses to the "bridge"—the walled heart, the protected mind, the cold, precise soul of the ship. There were brains there, large and small—not of flesh, but cybernetic brains of transistors and coils and wires, whose thought was a swift shuttling of electrons. They thought, now. With unhuman swiftness they evaluated the information, set up curves and plotted vectors on the computers, and reached their conclusion. Object: meteor. Course: collision.

The cold, limited, unhuman minds acted upon that conclusion at once. A message was flashed to relays, which sprang instantly alive. Throttles opened, the port lateral generators produced blasts of energy. The ship, moving at a velocity just under the speed of light, changed course—not a fraction too much, not a fraction too little.

The meteor went past, at a safe distance. The relays clicked again. The compensators hummed. There was another little burst of energy. On a master panel red needles on several dials crawled back until they were once more contact-aligned exactly with the black ones that monitored the course. The necessity for thought passed, the cold cybernetic brains ceased to think. And again, the all-pervading silence fell.

No passengers, no crew. But the ship carried a cargo. Ranked in the nether darkness, their atomic warheads pointing down the launching tubes, the missiles slept and waited, until their own relay systems should call them to go forth and fulfill themselves.

In the RSS-1, peace and no time.

In the *Liley B: Davenport*, far too much time and no peace at all.

Lying in his bunk Kirby tried to sleep and failed. From across the tiny cabin Shari's even breathing mocked him. She seemed to'be able to detach herself from her surroundings and exist undisturbed inside a kind of cocoon of patience that he envied but could not emulate. In the darkness, Kirby lit a cigarette and swore inaudibly, and felt old beyond Methuselah.

Time.

Chronometers. Calendars. Clocks. Days with no sunrise, nights with no moon. Arbitrary segments cut from a universal darkness, a formlessness, nothingness. Segments cut and shaped into little symbols and named with names that had no longer any meaning. What is Monday, in the spaces between the stars?

Time....

I should have done this when I was young, thought Kirby. I was sure of myself then. Now I don't know. I don't know at all. And I've get 'em here, the whole howling lot of 'em. Say the ether guys are to blame as much as I am, we were all in it together, made the plans and did the work and took the chances all the same—okay. But it all hung on a pilot, and that's me. Pop Barstow is too old. Joe Davenport—he was the start of it all, this was his ship and he hid her and kept her safe and started the whole plan—he's been dust on the Martian wind for years now. There aren't any young pilots any more, except the ones I've trained myself right here aboard. So it was up to me. I did it. If it hadn't been for me they'd all be sitting safe at home right now.

Time ....

Computers. You know your own velocity. You know the top potential of the R-ship. You know the distance. You figure as near as you can how long it takes to get that particular R-ship out of mothballs and in shape to go. You pare down even that interval, so as to be sure you're not giving yourself an edge you don't have. You feed all this stuff into the computer and you get an answer, and you still don't know. You can't be sure. It's too close. You just have to sit and wait and sweat and pray, and it's one hell of a feeling.

The cigarette was burned down to his fingers. He ground it out very carefully and reached for another, and then stopped. Pretty soon there would not be any more, but there was no use pushing it. Shari's peaceful breathing began to rasp on his nerves. He wanted to wake her up and make her sit and twitch with him, but he fought down that desire, too. Instead he got up and pulled on his pants and crept out without making any sounel. Outside in the corridor he stood for a moment trembling, thinking how it would be if anything happened to her. One in a million, she was. If they made it, if things worked out, they could still have kids. It wasn't too late....

Or was it? How close is that black shadow behind you in the void, the shadow you haven't seen nor heard but that you know is there, the swift shadow following?

He went forward to the bridge. Pop Barstow slumbered on the bench, and in the co-pilot's seat young Marapese, still too new to his responsibilities to be bored with them, sat rigidly erect, watching the banks of indicators that had said nothing too for far too long a time. Radarman Shaw sat in his cubby, half asleep. He needed a shave, and in repose his face bore the sulky expression of a child kept after school. Kirby walked over and kicked the bench hard under where Pop Barstow was lying.

"Hell of a watch you keep," he said.

Pop grunted and sat up, blinking at Kirby. "Too conscientious," he said. "That's the trouble with all you young fellows. Look." He pointed to Marapese, and then to Shaw. "What's the good of me staying awake too?"

"Because you're the senior officer," Kirby snarled. "Because it's customary. Because the kid's only a theoretical pilot as yet. Suppose something comes up he doesn't know how to deal with?"

"He'll wake me," said Pop reasonably. "You worry too much. That's bad. Ages a man before his time. Go back and get your sleep, Kirby. Anything happens, I'll let you know.

"All right, damn it, but stay awake!'

Kirby left the bridge. He started to go back to his cabin, but he had never felt less ready for sleep. He was tired, but there was a quivering restlessness on him, a sense of oppression. He did not know whether it was an honest presentiment or only the result of thinking too much about the same thing. Anyway, he couldn't go back in that dark little coop. He went instead to the hatch that led to the cargo deck.

It Was kept clossed. You couldn't have a bunch of kids swarming around the bridge, handling things. He opened it as quietly as he could and went down the ladder. It was dark below, except for A few dim lights. It was night time. You knew that because a bell rang and after a while the main lighting-tubes blinked off. Otherwise there was no change. There were no ports in the cargo deck, but if there had been it would have made no difference. What was outside had not altered since the day when, as a sort of afterthought, He made the stars also.

Kirby stood on the ladder and listened.

A child was crying, somewhere at the far end of the deck. People snored and turned and whimpered in their sleep. It was warm. The air was pure enough, but it had a stale flat taste from being breathed too many times and run through chemicals and across the hydroponic tanks. It smelled in here, of people and washing and food and babies—especially babies.

The child stopped crying. The muffled stirrings and sighings blended into a dim monotone. Kirby took hold of the iron rail. For some reason he had begun to shake. The air was heavy. The curtained cubicles wherein the families slept looked queer and shadowed in the dimness. The people were all hidden. There was not a human face. It was as though he stood alone, and underneath his feet the ship seemed weighted with a dreadful burden. Quite suddenly, Kirby turned and sprang up the ladder.

Shari was in the corridor. He thought she had been waiting for him beside the hatch. He looked at her and then past her, his eyes bright and hard, with an unnatural wideness.

"I'm going to turn back," he said.

"No."

"Damn it," he said roughly, "don't tell me no. I'm going back. I can't lead them all to the slaughter. I thought I could. I can't. We'll never make it. We haven't a chance in hell of making it."

"Kirby, listen. Don't be afraid now when it's too late. You had a great thought—"

"Who am I to have great thoughts? I'm nobody. I'm going back."

"Kirby—"

"Shut up. Don't argue with me." He was shaking all over, hard, and he couldn't stop. He had never felt like this before. It scared him. The iron walls of the corridor bent and wavered, and the deck moved under his feet. "I've got to get them back. I—"

"Kirby, they want you on the bridge." Her voice. Her quiet voice. Death, destruction, the hammer stroke, the end. He turned his head. There was no corridor now, no iron wall, the outer darkness had crept in and covered everything except her face. And it was pale and strange, and the eyes in it were shining.

He said in a voice that was not his own, but very softly, "They haven't called me,"

"They will,"

The whiteness and the blur that were Shari moved toward him and touched him with living lips, and his own flesh was cold, cold.

Someone was coming down the corridor, coming fast.

Kirby straightened up. The steps rang loud against the metal, a man's steps, running. Kirby waited.

It was Marapese. He was a young man and ashamed of fear, and he was trying not to show it, but when he spoke the words stumbled and stammered in his throat.

"Sir, Shaw says—" Pause. Tighten the lips and swallow and try again. "On the radar, sir—"

"All right." Kirby's voice was easy. It was confident, soothing, even jovial. He didn't know where it came from. He nodded to the hatch. "We don't have to tell them just yet. Shari, see about some coffee for us, will you? We'll be on the bridge." He put his hand on Marapese's shoulder. The hand was steady as a rock. It seemed not to be his own hand, but it was steady and it would do. The shoulder underneath It quivered. Kirby said, "Come on," He walked forward toward the bridge. He felt hollow inside, there was nothing to him but a shell, but no one would have known it to look at him. Marapese glanced side-long at him, a glance of worship. His own back bone stiffened and grew straight.

Behind them, Shari Smiled.

Kirby and the boy came into the bridge. Shaw was hunched over the scope. Pop Barstow stood with one hand on the pilot chair, his eyes riveted on Shaw, like one uncertain whether to go forward or back, and be was an old man.

Kirby had never realized before how truly old he was.

Shaw said, "It's still a long way off, but it's—" He hesitated. "—it."

"Yes," said Kirby. He glanced through the port of the inner bulkhead, into the space where the computers were. "That's all the good they were to us. We didn't even come close."

Pop Barstow said, in an unnaturally dry voice, "Too many variables. We were slower than we'd hoped. They were faster."

Marapese asked, "What do we do now?"

"We stop it," Kirby said, as though it were the simplest thing in the world.

Matapese stared at him. "Stop it?" he repeated. "Stop an R-ship?" He said it blankly, as in the past one might have said to a man standing on a railway track, top a locomotive?

Pop Barstow laughed, a laugh of unutterable sadness. "They have a plan," he said. "I've seen it. It's a pretty plan. It looks real good, all drawn up neat on a big white sheet of paper." He sat down in the pilot's seat and looked at Kirby. "You know what? We were crazy, and I was crazier than the rest of you. I was old enough to know better." He shook his head. "I'd have liked to live a while longer. Young folks think it doesn't matter to folks like me, but even when you're old you like living."

Kirby did not speak. He seemed to be thinking, very hard. Shaw squirmed and sweated over the radarscope. Marapese, very pale now, looked at them.

Shari came in with the coffee. Kirby looked up. Shari set the tray down, violently, so that the metal cups rattled.

"No," she said. "I couldn't do that, Kirby, it isn't the same—"

Kirby said slowly, "A cybernetic brain isn't so different from a human one. The principle is the same. It thinks."

The color had run out from under Shari's skin, leaving it ashen. "But you have seen, Kirby—I am only a little able, I could not do it—"

A, strange ruthlessness had risen in Kirby. "It might give us the edge we have to have. Pop's right the plan we've got is so much for the Birds, unless we add something to it.

Marapese Stared at Shari's stricken face, not understanding. But Pop Barstow understood, and was shaken. "It seems creepy," he muttered, "but it might do it—it might—"

Kirby said to Shaw, "Keep tracking it. We need an absolutely accurate check on course and velocity. I'm going down to get Wilson and Krejewski." He thought, "And oh God, I've got to tell them all, and when those women start screaming—"

He got the surprise of his life, when he went below and told them. He spoke as casually as he could to Wilson, and to Krejewski who had spent his adult life building and repairing R-ships, and to Weiss, who had been a junior assistant in Cybernetic Division. He spoke, and braced himself for the outcry.

It came—but it was only one solitary wail from Sally Wilson, followed immediately by a smack from Mrs. Krejewski. "They have to do it, she told Sally. "Don't make it any harder for them." Then she turned to Kirby. "Just don't come back without my George, that's all." Kirby looked into her eyes and thought that if anything did happen to George it had better happen to him, too. It would be easier.

He Herded his three lagging heros up the ladder and back to the bridge, still stunned by the unexpected ease of something he had dreaded. Pop Barstow grinned a little. "I told you you didn't understand women, Kirby. They'll make your life miserable over little things, but when something really big comes along they surprise you." He nodded. "Look at Shari." Kirby looked. Her face was pale, but no longer stricken. "Still afraid?" he asked her.

"Yes. But I see that I have to try. And I would rather go with you than stay behind. She added, very earnestly, "Don't trust in me too much. I don't know that it can be done at all, and if it can, I don't know whether I will read it right."

"You'll be okay. Pop, take them along, get them ready, and give everything a final double-check. Everything. Take your time, don't hurry it. I've got to work out the timing and the course."

He turned to Shaw, and ultimately to the computers. Velocity of *Lucy B, Davenport*, so much. Velocity of R-ship, so much. Differential. Rate of approach. Course of *Lucy B. Davenport*. Course of R-ship, which cannot possibly fire its missiles ahead of it because it's already traveling at absolute top under the speed of light and has therefore to parallel and head the slower ship, releasing its missiles on a reverse arc. Relative position of two ships now, plus mean distance on plane of flight, plus potential velocity of life-skiff, plus estimated relative position of—

You plot parallelograms on nothing, you look at the figures and they are not realities. The realities are Nemesis, and fear, and human beings trapped in an iron trap, and folly, and a dream.

You plot the parallelogram, and it is only the beginning. The R-ship is intelligent. It is wary. It will not permit a skiff, or a man, or a chunk of cosmic drift to get close to it. The sensor field provides a barrier, a defense impossible to penetrate. So you think again and figure again. You extend the short line in the parallelogram that is the projected course of the life-skiff, and you add to it so many degrees of arc after it heads the still unfinished long line that is the course of the approaching R-ship. And then you bend that long line inward and then outward again in a swift apex, and you make a circle at that apex, a circle on nothing which will enclose the lives of Wilson and Weiss and Krejewski, of Shari and yourself. And if you have not forgotten how, you pray.

When there is no more value in either figuring or prayer, you rise and go.

The corridor seemed curiously foreshortened. There seemed no distance at all between the bridgeroom and the place where the port life-skiff housed, an embryo in an iron womb. The others were already inside it. Pop helped Kirby on with his space suit.

"Everything's right," Pop said. "I checked real careful. All the tools and stuff."

Kirby looked down at the bulky suit. "I hoped we wouldn't have to use these things. Oh, well Put Fenner on the radio and see he keeps it wide open. I want contact all the way."

He climbed into the skiff, and took the controls. The lock sealed. A roar, a grinding, a whistle and a leaping shock, and they were free. The booster jets howled, briefly doubling the normal rocket thrust to break the gravitational pull of the mother ship.

Behind Kirby, Shari sat very rigid. Kirby paid no attention to them. He was too scared himself. He set his course, repeating the coordinates over aloud. He had Wilson check them too, just to be on the safe side.

"Kirby." Wilson's voice was a little raw. Kirby, why did they have to drive us to this. They're only human, like us."

"Yes, but they're dedicated to a status quo. If we licked the R-ships and made it to a new world, too many people would want to follow."

Wilson sard, "But we'd be too far away to bother *them*. Why—"

Kirby shook his head. "Nothing stays too far away forever. Forget about it. Shut up."

The skiff rushed on, making the first leg of its appointed course. The rockets drummed. Kirby glared at the indicators. The others sat in silence, in agony, in solid dread.

Presently Kirby said, "Time. Secure your helmets and check oxygen flow. Everybody's audio working? Okay." He switched on the small but very powerful communication unit built into the suit and spoke briefly to Fenner aboard the *Lucy Davenport*. "Clear both ways. One of us will be in contact with you from now on. We're going out now."

Wilson let out one sound that might have been a sob.

Kirby cut in the starboard laterals, throttled down to one-quarter maximum thrust. Moving fast now, he saw that the space-line was secure, the long line that strung the four, men and one woman together like bundles on a cord. "Get your hand rockets ready," he said, "but be damned careful how you fire them!" He added, with- a last-minute touch of gentleness, "Don't worry. I've done this before. It's not so different from an ordinary space-jump for salvage."

He threw over the lever. The small lock opened and spewed them out.

V

Kirby's heart came up and hit him under the chin and the enormous vault of stars reeled and wheeled around him, and his helmet audio was filled with the sounds of anguish from the four other shapes that rolled and sprawled and kicked in the unthinkable void.

"Get those rockets working!" Kirby, bellowed. The five hand rockets flared raggedly and then all together. The combined push was enough. The little skiff went on away from them, alone and empty, beginning its long curve toward its find destiny.

"Just take it easy,'" Kirby ssid. "Relax. You can't possibly fall."

Not possibly. There's no place to fall to. There's nothing here, nothing. You wonder why He made so much space and never used it ....

Man wasn't made for this. Man was born and bred for a million years on a planet, He needs solid ground under his feet. Or else he needs the illusion of it, an iron deck, a shell to close him in so his littleness looks its normal size, so he doesn't shrink and vanish and become no more than a tiny unheard shriek in a vastness where even the stars are small.

Courage. A man is supposed to have it. But where do you go to look for it when it's dropped out somewhere in the darkness where no sun shines?

"Kirby—"

"Kirby!"

"KIRBY!"

"What do you want? You're all right. All you have to do is wait."

"But Kirby..."

"I tell you we're okay, on time, in the right place, We can't miss."

Can't we? Were the calculations right? Will the R-ship swerve the way we want it to, or will it do something unexpected, something clever, and uncanny? It isn't right for a ship to fly itself, to think and feel as though if were alive and on it's own out here, Pluto base is too far away for any contact now. All by itself. It isn't right.

Wish they had lights, like human ships. Hard to see one black blot against half the blackness of the inverse. His eyes ached, looking into nothing, at nothing he was sick, and very cold. Voices spoke, and one of them was Shari's, and...

Did that star wink out?

A flicker. Another. A red streak. That's it, that's the latera's of the R-ship, its sensor-field has picked up the skiff curving round on the far side, and the so-and-so is swerving ....

A thin voice cried, "It's coming right into us!"

Kirby shouted. Orders, prayers, curses. Not many, there wasn't time. A black shape loomed. It did not seem, in that weird and silent gulf, to be moving. It merely grew, without sound or rush or roar. It was small. It grew and was large. It was enormous. It was close beside them.

It's sensed us, but it's overrun its ability. It can't swerve two ways at once. Fast, now. Make it fast. There won't be any other chances, and this is no place to be left behind!

Hand-rockets. Tiny sparks in the overwhelming All. Magnetic grapples, clanging hard on the dark cold metal, only there is no clang, its as quiet as a deaf man's dream, and there are stars over and under and all around, except where the solid blackness is beneath your feet.

It's swerving again, to get away from these five little intruders into its sensor-field. There is still no sense of motion but you can feel the change of direction. The grapple lines come taut. Old man inertia again, but this time he isn't big enough and a burst from the hand-rockets takes care of him. The lines slack again, the magnetic plates on your iron boots bite strongly. You have outwitted an R-ship. It is a triumph few men have achieved.

Few men? None, until now.

You are weak. The blood, the bone, the guts have run out of you. You merely cling, and stare at the emptiness where you might so easily have been left, and tell Fenner inanely over the radio, "We made it."

The hull shuddered slightly. Kirby thought; "It's trying to shake us off, like a dog!" A wave of superstitious horror lifted the hair on his head and then he saw the space-suit that had Weiss' name on pointing astern where a slim torpedo shape had begun with a dignified terrible deliberation.

"It's taking care of the skiff," Weiss said.

"Yeah," said Kirby. "Okay, Krejewski, Wilson—it's your show. Take over."

Shari had been silent, very silent since they had begun their clinging to the dark hull. Now she spoke, saying Kirby's name hesitantly.

"Are you getting anything?"

"I—don't know. Something. Cold and strange. It's not like human thought at all. Very cold, and clear like one single note, if I could only read it....I think It knows we're here."

"The sensor-field would have told it that," said Weiss. "It sends all the data on everything it touches to the cybernetic control center in the bridge, where the information is correlated and—"

"I think," said Shari, "It hates us."

Again the chill of superstition crept and crawled in Kirby's nerves. He said angrily, "Don't go imagining things. It's only a machine. It can't feel"

"I suppose it can, in a way," Weiss said slowly. "As a safeguard against sabotage, against just what we're doing now. They're built that way, to regard humans as a menace. All their power has to be cut off before we can get in the ships on the ground, to service them."

Kirby growled, "Three experts and a telepath ought to be able to out-guess one lousy mechanical brain."

Wilson and Krejewskj had been unhooking the cutting-torches from their belts. Wilson said nervously, "Might as well cut in here as anywhere. We'd never crack the doors. But remember these things have got automatic repair-devices, so get in fast when we hole through. Now stand clear."

Out in the void that they had left behind bright period to his words, a flare lit up the eternal night, burned savagely, and was gone.

"There goes the skiff. We're starting cutting. Keep clear!"

The rest moved back to the limit of their slack on the long line. The small hypnotic flicker of the ato-flames ate away at the metal.

Kirby questioned Shari. She only answered, in a remote queer voice, "it's still—thinking."

Krejewski suddenly yelled as the metal they were cutting bulged up under them. The lines snapped taut as the others pulled them back, and there was suddenly a big ragged hole in the ship's flank. And the ship stirred inwardly, as though it could feel the wound, as though the fine-drawn nerves of titanum that threaded all its bulk were carrying a message of pain.

Krejewski grunted, "Air blew out. The interior compartments will seal off automatically. Air pressure and temperature have to be kept constant—these sensitive gadgets won't do well in a vacuum at absolute zero—"

"Quit gabbling and get in" Wilson cried.

Kirby thrust himself into the hole. The knife edged beam of his belt lamp slashed into the blackness, picking out the enormous ribs of the ship, touching a network of steel struts and braces.

Shari said abruptly, "Something is coming. The—the brain of the ship has sent it—it doesn't think for itself, I don't know What it is."

"An automatic welder, to patch this hole," said Wilson. "Hurry!"

Kirby glimpsed something moving in that interior darkness. He pulled with all his strength on the rope that linked him to Weiss. A flash of Weiss' belt lamp lit the thing that was coming, a thing moving ponderously on gliding bands of magnetized metal, a huge distorted spider crawling toward the hole.

Weiss came through, with Shari's feet almost on his shoulders. They were pushing each other from outside now, in a panic. Shari was in and Wilson came through with three pairs of hands hauling hard, and Wilson pulled frantically on Krejewski's boots.

"The things stopped," shrilled Weiss. "Right at the edge of the hole, right beside us."

It's measuring, Kirby thought. Give it a second or two to determine the size of the hole, and—damn these robots! Damn every one that was ever made, right back to thermostats and self-turning-off ovens. Men ought never to have surrendered to machines. What the hell's keeping Krejewski? I never knew he was thirty feet high.

It only seemed that way. Actually, Krejewski popped in like a cork from a bottle, but he had no time to throw away. The calculations circuits in the welder had finished their computation. From out of its unlovely body it produced a steel plate of the proper size and clapped it over the hole, clearing Krejewski's helmet by less than a foot. He was barely out of range of the backlash when the welding flames went into action.

They worled their way in to the catwalk and clung there, watchmg while the inexorable machine welded them securely inside the R-ship. No one mentioned that. Their thoughts were too unpleasant for utterance.

Finished with its duty, the welder moved away, returning to whatever place it occupied in the dark silence of the hull when it was not needed. Krejewski muttered, "Wait until the air is replaced in this section. That'll unseal the bulkhead doors."

They waited. Kirby's heart was pounding fast and hard. He was sweating inside his suit. Presently the hard-edged lamp-beams softened and diffused. There was air again. He opened his helmet. The air was warm, stale, unused, unbreathed, tainted with unhuman smells of metal and oil and plastics and hot glass.

Shari's face emerged from the obscurity. "It knows we're here inside it," she whispered.

"Kirby, it *does* hate us—not as a man would hate, I've seen hate and it comes hot and bright into the mind, a red thing like fire—this is different. This is cold. Dark. It's not living, and yet it is. It knows how to destroy us, and it will."

"Can you see how?" asked Kirby eagerly,

She whimpered, and he thought she was going to weep. "If I were not so frightened, if I could keep my own mind clear—" With shocking suddenness she did break into tears. "I told you I was not good enough for this, not to depend on me!"

"There was no one else," said Kirby quietly. "You can do it, if you really try."

She did not answer, and he did not know what she was thinking now. The light was better now, with the air diffusing the glare of the lamps. Aft and forward ran the catwalks, and the arching braces, and the walls of gleaming metal. It was not like a ship. It was not made for men. The catwalks were the one small concession to them.

Kirby said, "We'd better get a move on."

Krejewski pointed. "It—what we're after is up in the bridge."

They tried to hurry, but in that almost zero-gravity they moved like swimmers in deep water, floating, stumbling. The catwalks were floored with a yielding plastic tile, no good for magnetized boots. They seemed to be fumbling their way through a brooding metal labyrinth, dark, silent.

Kirby had a nightmare vision of failure, of four men and a woman trapped and dying slowly in an unmanned ship that would bear their bodies back to Sol as mute evidence of a mission accomplished. He dreaded each moment to hear the lateral rockets begin, to know that they had headed the *Lucy B. Davenport* and that it was too late.

"If we'd tried for the torpedoes," Wilson mumbled. "Maybe, if we could have fired them off—"

"They're locked in tight," Weiss' voice retorted. "And even without them, the ship could have been used to ram the *Lucy*."

"They can't have it under control now, not at all this distance!"

"They don't have to! The pattern of its mission was set up for it, and the alternative methods of achieving it. The little cams and buttons will do the rest."

"Shut up and bring that torch here," Kirby said. "Quick."

He was at the bridgeroom door, and it was closed and locked. A key back at Pluto base would open it, but nothing else but brute force would.

The torch bit into the metal. Wilson muttered, as he played it, "Never been up this high before. Nobody but the top cyberneticists rated access to the bridge. I wonder—

"Don't wonder."

The lock, burned through, grated and sagged. Kirby pushed the door open.

"Listen, what's that?"

Kirby had heard it too, the snick of metal and a soft humming. The humming kept on.

He was looking into darkness. There were no windows in this bridgeroom. The mariner who navigated here had surer senses than sight.

He swung his lamp. They looked at the thing.

There was an odd relief about seeing it. One had almost imagined a great figure, a monstrous metallic face, a something—

Here was just a machine. Humans had made it, humans had given it its orders. That was all. Just like the calculating machines that were so familiar these days—the tall bank of transistor-cells, the deceptively simple wiring, the shielded power leads, the vernier dials for wave settings.

No metal face, no staring eyes, nothing humanoid or menacing, nothing but a machine that humans had made and humans could smash up. He lifted his heavy wrench and started forward.

"Kirby, wait!"

Shari's voice had something in it he'd never heard. That, rather than the warning in her words, stopped him.

"There's danger," she said. "Wait. Don't go. I can get it—I can almost get it. It's waiting, something warned it of our approach, it's—"

"Oh, hell," said Wilson.

"I'm not hysterical!" she cried. "It's hard to explain, I get it just over the limits of consciousness, but this—this thing—it's *prepared*."

Kirby felt the hairs lift on the back of his neck. "Keep back," he told them. "Give me room to swing."

He swung the heavy wrench and hurled it at the dialed face, What happened, happened fast.

The wrench, a yard from the dials, flew back at them with a flash of light. Weiss screamed. There was a metallic clang. Then silence.

"It hit me—I think my forearm's broken!" cried Weiss.

"It threw the wrench back at us," said Wilson, his voice hoarse. "Like—like—"

Kirby got control of his own feelings. "Listen. There's a force-field around it. It came on automatically when we broke in. Of course. It came on to protect it, for only intruders would break in."

"But we can't get through that," Krejewski said. "There's no way," "So we're licked?'"

Then; suddenly a sweet, high-pitched note-of sound sang from the tall metal bank of cells. Nothing else—no movement, no lights.

But, instantly, there came the low rumble of the port laterals firing.

Kirby, at the first vibration of that rumbling thunder, dived toward the others.

They were in a group back of him. He knocked them staggering toward the door opening, Weiss yelling as his arm hit something. Their tangled little group wedged against the door, The ship canted sharply. It moved in a turn too sharp for any human crew to endure, but perfectly practicable for a ship that had no crew. It crushed them against the doorframe, Kirby desperately holding Shari.

The rumble of rockets stopped. The pressure relaxed. Weiss was sobbing from pain.

"Damn near threw us into that forcefield," Wilson was saying. "Let's get out of this!" He scrambled panically away.

Kirby hauled him back. "Get out, to where? To empty space? Not to the ark—it won't exist, if we leave here now! This R-ship is starting to head around. Do you understand that? It's altering course, and that means it'll soon be launching its warheads at the ark. Unless we stop it!"

"But how? We can't get near it—we can't touch it—how?"

Kirby swore. He looked at the thing that lay so securely beyond their reach. He hated it. It was the symbol and the force of the power that had enchained mankind. It was everything that he and the others on the ark had fought and fled from, and it had won, reaching even here into the emptiness between the stars to grasp at human aspiration and make it not. A great rage rose up in him.

"Weiss, you're the cybernetics man. Dammit, stop blubbering and listen to me! We can't smash it up by brute force—okay. Isn't there another way? Men build these things. They can't be smarter than men. They can't be all-powerful."

Weiss answered wearily, "They might as well be as far as we're concerned. Even if we knew the frequency and the code that controls this particular ship, it wouldn't do us any good. See that master panel? It's different from any other I've seen, designed especially for a star-ship that has to be out of touch with its base, on its own. It's locked. Nothing's going to change the settings on it until the orders they represent have been carried out. Then they' ll shift into the 'Return to Base' position. And that's that."

"It has an order," Kirby said. "It can't disobey that order." He was fishing for an idea, a nebulous thing out of human psychology remembered from a lot of long dark years. Suddenly he took Weiss by the shoulders. "These cybernetic brains aren't very different from the human variety are they?"

"No. look out, you're hurting my arm. Simpler, of course, faster reaction time on a lot of things, only subliminal 'emotional' complications—no, they're not too different."

"Weiss, you and Wilson are going to figure out from watching its reactions what wave-length the thing is sensitive to. And you've got no time to do it in. Fenner, stand by with every amp you've got. Give me a scatter band in the UH frequencies, the banned-off ones." The ark's communicator had been built before the banning, before there was no longer any need for ships to talk together across space. Near a control center it would have been drowned out by the vastly more powerful transmitter, but here in this untracked waste of nothingness it might work. It might.

"Watch it," he said to the two men hanging irresolute in the doorway. "Switch in, and give your readings direct to Fenner."

"Kirby," said Wilson, "you're crazy. But I guess it doesn't matter now. I'm sorry we all did this thing, though. I should have stayed on Mars. I don't want Sally and the kids to die. I don't want to die myself."

Kirby hit him, clumsily, savagely, across the back. "Then watch it, damn you! *There!*"

A bank of transistors that had been dark glowed briefly, and were dark again. Weiss began to talk, very fast, very nervous, to Fenner. Kirby got busy with the space-line. There were railings on the catwalk. He threw hitches over them, made himself and the others fast so they couldn't be pitched forward into that deadly room, or smashed against the struts. He took Shari in his arms and said to Krejewski, "Hang on. If this works, it'll be rough."

"Narrow it down," Weiss was saying. "What have you got there? No, you lost it again. Higher. That's it. I think. Oh, God, my arm hurts. No, no, Fenner, try it again! slower, hold it—it's receiving now but it isn't reacting, what good is the frequency without the code word? It could be anything. Run through the alphabet, fast. May. be we—"

Again that one sweet note, and the following thunder of the laterals. Again the terrible hand of inertia struck them, crushed them, left them dazed and gasping.

"Hurry it up," said Kirby. "Hurry." Wilson wept and cursed him. Weiss, half conscious in the doorway, was muttering his ABC's.

"M, N, O—no reaction yet, go on—P, Q, R, S—S! Hold it, Fenner. There was a flicker on S. It's waiting for the rest of the word. The rest of the word. There's a million of 'em beginning with S."

"Try STAR," said Kirby.

It didn't work.

It was Fenner who suggested STELLA.

It worked.

"Pour it on," Kirby shouted. "Tell it to sheer off, change course. Fast, FAST,"

The receiving unit glowed and a humming, soft and busy, arose in the relays of the brain.

"Hang on."

This time it was the starboard laterals. Krejewski and Wilson yelled together in mingled anguish and delight. Weiss had fainted. Kirby, holding tight to Shari and enduring the pressure, did not exult. The burst was short. Almost at once the port laterals roared again. The locked master control and the compensators were not to be defeated so lightly. The RSS-1 was back on course again.

"Keep it coming," Kirby said. "Tell it to return to base. Ten it to by-pass its master circuit, I don't suppose it can, but it might confuse it." Past Wilson's crouching shape he could see the glow and flicker of the banked transistor. Cerebration, naked and visible. It still seemed like witchcraft to Kirby. Fenner's voice spoke in his ears, remote and twanging like a tuat wire. "It's getting awful close to us—what's it doing there?" Kirby could feel him sweating.

The starboard laterals swung the ship over in a vicious arc. Kirby braced himself. "It's beating us to death," he gasped, "but that's alright, that's what I want—" One breath, one burst of speech before the compensators took over.

Krejewski whispered, "We can't take much more of this."

"Pour it on, Fenner. Return to base—"

Shari, who sagged in his arms like a limp rag doll, lifted he head and said, "It's confused, it—" She quivered, seizing his wrist with desperate hands. "Kirby, hold me, I'm afraid!"

Thunder. Chaos. Pressure, vertigo, a gasping and a straining and a cry, five small soft humans crushed and trapped between titanic forces. The laterals boomed and kicked, fighting each other, hurling the ship into a mad pinwheel flight, across nothing, to nowhere. Kirby, blinded, deafened, barely conscious, screeched triumphantly, "Pour it on!" The darkness was full of sound.

In the bridgeroom, in the brain, something blew.

Convulsion, the throes of death. Crazy, it can't be dying, it never lived. It's only an iron hull, a cold hulk, soulless. Why does it kick and lash itself about like a living thing in pain? Oh, no, oh, God, stop it, I can't stand it any longer, my own agony is too great!

Hear the strands of its brain parting? Hear the snap and the anguished tearing? It's only glass and metal. It can't feel. Shari, don't, stop wailing. Shari—

Suddenly, it is very still.

The ship is dead.

Shari is still weeping. "It was bewildered, it couldn't understand. Kirby, it knew, and at the end it was afraid. It was afraid of its own madness."

Crazy., It wasn't human. But wasn't it a. human trick you played on it? Give it order it can't obey, impulses it can't satisfy, and what happens? What happens to the infinitely more complex, more flexible ana reasoning brain of a man, when it is tortured with conflicting problems it can't solve? It splits wide open. The doctors have a name for it. Schizophrenia.

It's dead, and the ship is only a plunging wreck.

Kirby got up. He freed himself from the rope and stumbled forward over the squirming, groaning bodies of men who were, miraculously, still alive to groan. It was silent in the bridgeroom. It had always been silent, but now there was no presence in it. He got his hands on something and threw it. It crashed with a bursting tinkle into the master panel, where the dial settings remained unaltered, inexorable in authority. Kirby laughed. The force-field was gone. He picked up the wrench that had broken Weiss' arm. For a moment he ceased to be Kirby, or any other man. He was rebellion. He was all the people in the ark. He was the people who would follow them in other ships. He was the might and the power of his kind, trampling and smashing and wrecking with insensate joy the might and power of the dark ships. He was humanity. He was triumph.

He didn't know that he was any of these things. The wrench dropped out of his hands. He was exhausted and his battered body hurt. He walked slowly out of the bridgeroom, his boots crunching on broken glass. "Come on," he said. "Come on, you guys, we've still got to cut our way out of this." Into the radio, to Fenner, hysterical on the ether end, he said only, "We licked it. Tell Pop to come over and pick us up,"

Ahead, the way to the stars was clear. Behind them, for better or worse on the far-flung worlds of Sol, the day of the robot ships had begun its end."Kirby roused up his army of four, and stumbled away along the catwalk in the silence and the dark.